MARY HANSON

The Difference Between Babies & Cookies

Illustrated by **Debbie Tilley**

Silver Whistle · Harcourt, Inc.
San Diego   New York   London

www.harcourt.com

Silver Whistle is a trademark of Harcourt, Inc.,
registered in the United States of America and/or other jurisdictions.

Library of Congress Cataloging-in-Publication Data
Hanson, Mary Elizabeth.
The difference between babies & cookies/Mary Hanson; illustrated by Debbie Tilley.
p. cm.
"Silver Whistle."
Summary: A child's mother compares babies to such things as cookies, puppies, bread, tiger cubs, and sunshine.
[1. Babies—Fiction.]   I. Tilley, Debbie, ill.   II. Title.
PZ7.H1988Di   2002
[E]—dc21   00-8447
ISBN 0-15-202406-9

First edition
A C E G H F D B

Printed in Mexico

The illustrations in this book were prepared with watercolor paint.
The display and text type were set in Big Dog.
Color separations by Bright Arts Ltd., Hong Kong

This book was printed on totally chlorine-free Nymolla Matte Art paper.
Production supervision by Sandra Grebenar and Ginger Boyer
Designed by Carolyn Stafford

For my own cookies, Allie and Michael

— M. H.

For Gillian

— D. T.

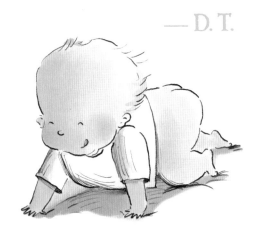

Before my little sister was born, my mom tried
to teach me about babies.

I listened carefully, but it's not as easy as you might think.
Even my mom gets mixed up sometimes....

Mom said babies are as sweet as cookies.

But I learned that you cannot **dip them in milk.**

Mom said babies are as cuddly as puppies.

They drool more.

Mom said babies are as hungry as bears.

Unless you feed them mooshed peas.

Mom said babies' cheeks are as rosy as apples.

You can't give your sister to your teacher.

Mom said babies are as wiggly as worms.

Do *not* try to catch fish with them.

Mom said babies smell like whipped cream.

Mom said babies are as playful as tiger cubs.

It's definitely not okay to paint stripes on them.

Mom said babies are as soft and warm as fresh-baked bread.

They get slippery when you butter them.

Mom said babies are like sunshine on a rainy day.

Especially when they're covered in mud.

Mom said babies are gifts from the angels.

It's a good thing she likes surprises.

I don't know where Mom gets this stuff.

I'm just glad I'm here to help take care of our baby.
She shouldn't grow up thinking she's a cookie.